The Suffering of Innocents

By Marc Zirogiannis

The Suffering of Innocents
Copyright © 2015 by Marc Zirogiannis.
All rights reserved.

No part of this publication may be reproduced, stored in a retrieval system or transmitted in any way by any means, electronic, mechanical, photocopy, recording or otherwise, without the prior permission of the author except as provided by USA copyright law.

All characters appearing in this work are fictitious. Any resemblance to real persons, living or dead, is purely coincidental.

The opinions expressed by the author are not necessarily those of Revival Waves of Glory Books & Publishing.

Published by Revival Waves of Glory Books & Publishing
PO Box 596| Litchfield, Illinois 62056 USA
www.revivalwavesofgloryministries.com

Revival Waves of Glory Books & Publishing is committed to excellence in the publishing industry.

Book design copyright © 2015 by Revival Waves of Glory Books & Publishing. All rights reserved.

Inquiries or additional information, contact:

Marc A. Zirogiannis
338 Jericho Turnpike-Ste 114
Syosset, NY 11791
Email: redflagadvisors@gmail.com

Or visit

http://marczirogiannis.webs.com

For Soraya

About the Author

Marc Zirogiannis holds a B.A. from Long Island University and a *Juris Doctor* from Hofstra University's School of Law. Mr. Zirogiannis is a world renowned Business Development Consultant and Author. Mr. Zirogiannis has practiced the martial arts for over 25 years and earned a 2nd Dan under the supervision of Grandmaster Yeon Hwan Park in Levittown, New York. He has been active in practicing and teaching meditation for 10 years. He has published numerous books, eBooks, and Audio Books and on a variety of subjects, and, is currently the lead correspondent for **Tae Kwon Do Times**, an international print publication. He lectures on a variety of topics, including business development, personal development, and matters of the martial arts. His last novella, **Hitler's Orphan: Demetri of Kalavryta,** has won critical acclaim and been the subject of a radio program. It is currently in negotiations to become the basis of a more extensive work.

Acknowledgements

Endless thanks for the love and support of my beloved Soraya, and my boys, DJ, Deme, Joseph and Sebastian. Without them it all means nothing.

This book is dedicated to Father Eugene Pappas for challenging the mind with thought provoking topics on his weekly radio show in NYC.

This book is a work of fiction that evokes certain negative images of the characters featured. It is not an attempt to discredit any real individuals or institutions.

This book is a work of fiction. Names, characters, places, and incidents either are products of the author's imagination or are used fictitiously. Any resemblance to actual persons, living or dead, events, or locales is entirely coincidental.

-Marc Zirogiannis

Table of Contents

Chapter 1 1
Chapter 2 4
Chapter 3 8
Chapter 4 10
Chapter 5 14
Chapter 6 19
Chapter 7 22
Chapter 8 28
Chapter 9 32
Chapter 10 38
Chapter 11 45
Chapter 12 50
Chapter 13 57
Chapter 14 63
Chapter 15 65

Chapter 1

"Why Do The Righteous Suffer?" (**The Book of Job**)

Sam Job awoke that morning, as he did most mornings, filled with hope and joy. While he didn't always say the words out loud, or even to himself, his mindset was one of genuine appreciation.

"Thank you Lord for all you have given me. Thanks you for my beautiful wife, my wonderful children. Thank you for our health and relative prosperity. Thank you for my success."

For Sam these were not just empty words. He really was thankful. He had met his wife, Laura, in college. There was an instant chemistry between them, although she played *"hard to get"* for a long time before breaking down and going on a dinner date with him. That was the night that started it all.

Now, twenty-five years later, they were married with three children, a house in the suburbs, and two flourishing careers. Most importantly, they were still very much in love with each other. They still found ways to make each other laugh. They still found time for romantic intimacy. For Sam his passion for Laura got even stronger over the years. The more he loved her the more he desired her. He knew she was aware of it. He probably loved and desired her more than she him. That was okay by him.

This morning, like he did every Tuesday, it was his turn to drop off and pick up the twins from daycare. Tuesday was always Laura's longest day of the workweek. Sam had somewhat more flexibility in his work schedule. The law firm where he worked for the past eight years never gave him a hard time about his family obligations. He was a beloved member of the firm.

Everyone at his office knew Tuesday was his day for the kids. They were happy to oblige. He enjoyed spending the extra time with the kids and he felt good about being able to make his beautiful wife's life easier.

As he came down the stairs of their modest split level home and finished knotting his necktie he caught a glimpse of her bent over, unloading the dishwasher. He snuck up behind her and wrapped his arms around her waist and kissed her neck from behind.

"*Morning baby,*" he said.

"*Morning Sam.*" "*Say good morning to Daddy.*"

"*Morning Daddy,*" the twins said in unison.

Jonah and Noah were fraternal twins. They were four years old. Both were terrific boys, but they had very different personalities. Jonah was much more serious and organized, even for a four year old. He got that from his Mom. Noah was the clown. He was always joking and getting into mischief. They had a strong bond with each other and they were very close. These boys, and their older brother, were everything to Sam and Laura.

"*Sammy made it off okay?*" He asked, referring to their oldest, the sixteen year old.

"*He is a crabby pain in the ass.*"

"*Mommy, you said a bad word!*" Jonah admonished.

"*That's enough, Jonah. You guys finish eating. We are going to be late.*"

With that Laura kissed everyone and started gathering her stuff for work. She zipped her briefcase closed and strapped it over her right shoulder. With the same hand she grabbed the travel mug containing her second cup of hot coffee. She was a matrimonial attorney for a small but highly regarded firm located on the Island. She was dressed in a skirt and matching suit jacket. She looked professional, but you could still make out the outline of her amazing figure.

"Bye guys. Be good for Daddy. I will see you tonight. Be sure to remind the teacher that I don't want them napping. They never sleep when they do."

"Okay. Have a good day."

"Text me after you drop them." The door closed behind her and she was off.

"Okay guys. Get your shoes and jackets on."

"Is this the right foot?" Jonah asked.

"Yes, that is correct. Noah, what's the hold up?"

"I farted," Noah replied and then he and Jonah both burst into raucous laughter.

"Don't say that. It's not nice. Now put your shoes on silly."

Shoes were on. Jackets were zippered. Backpacks were mounted on their small backs as they left the house and jumped into the back of Sam's new Ford Escape and headed to their daycare for a day coloring, counting, socializing and whatever else it is kids do during the course of a day in a daycare program.

Chapter 2

The clock struck 4:00PM as Sam finished loading his briefcase with whatever work he was taking home for the evening. He wasn't really able to pay too much attention to what he was doing because his head had been pounding for two hours straight. He took some aspirin and an Advil, but they provided no relief. In fact, it was getting worse, not better. Then he remembered that he had some Percs in his desk drawer from his oral surgery. He popped two of those in his mouth and washed them down quickly with some water before racing for the elevator. He needed to get the boys before 5:00PM.

When Sam pulled up in front of the Sunshine Daycare it was about five minutes to 5:00PM. His head was still pounding. He raced up the walkway to the front door, which was locked for security reasons, and pressed the buzzer.

"Who is it?" a familiar female voice asked.

"It's Sam. I am here for the terrors."

"They are angels," the voice responded as the audible buzzing of the door rang out.

Sam opened the door and walked silently around the corner to the boys' classroom. He loved to catch an unsuspecting glimpse of the twins at play to see how they were adjusting and socializing in their daycare environment. He really never liked the idea of the kids in daycare to begin with. He wanted the kids to be with Laura until they started kindergarten. They even fought about it, a little, but he understood that Laura going back to work was good for her and good for the family. He also knew that getting an early start on socializing with other kids and more structured education would be good for two kids who were so smart. In the end it was a great decision for everyone. Laura was thriving, as were the boys. When Laura and the kids did well Sam, naturally, did well too. Laura was kind about only an occasional "*I told you so.*"

As he peered through the classroom window unnoticed, he saw Noah seated by himself at a long table coloring in a Spider-Man coloring book. He loved Spider-Man. His part of the room that he shared with his brother was all decked out in a Spider-man theme. Spider-Man coloring books. Spider-Man pajamas. Spider-Man snacks. Spider-Man toys. He couldn't get enough of the web-slinging, wall-crawling super-hero.

Jonah was leading some game with the few remaining boys and girls whose parents hadn't picked them up yet. He was providing some kind of unintelligible instructions to the other children as they formed a circle. Unintelligible to Sam, but the kids seemed to understand the orders with no need for clarity at all.

"*Daddy's here!*" Noah screamed with delight at catching a glimpse of Sam in the window. His cover was blown, but that was okay. He had seen enough to give him comfort and joy. He turned the door handle and entered the classroom.

"*Hi boys. How was your day?*"

"*Good*" they both shouted.

They then proceeded with their daily routine of cleaning up their play areas. This was followed by a march to their respective cubbies to put on their jackets and backpacks. Jonah went and hugged the teacher goodbye, as he always did, and Noah, simply, waved. They made their way down the hall and out the same door Sam had entered the school, with the boys in a sizeable lead ahead of their father.

"Hold hands guys. DO NOT GO IN THE STREET!" Sam hollered as the boys approached the car. The parking near the school was limited, so he had no choice but to pull in front of the daycare, on the busy street. His solution, actually Laura's solution, was to get both boys to enter the car from the passenger side. This was a safer solution than worrying about one straying into an oncoming car.

Sam opened the rear passenger door and the boys entered the vehicle single file, Noah first, Jonah behind. Noah was slightly smaller so he drew the short straw. He got the privilege of sitting behind the driver's seat while Jonah had the freedom to stretch his legs behind an empty front passenger seat. Sam would have had them switch once and awhile for the sake of equity, but not for Jonah's fixation on routine. He didn't like unnecessary change. To avoid the unnecessary whining associated with the unnecessary change Sam obliged him with assigned seats in the car.

Sam buckled Jonah into his booster seat and then walked around the rear of the car to the rear passenger seat and attempted to buckle Noah who had already made his way to the front seat. He was turning the steering wheel of the car, pretending to drive.

"Come on Noah. We gotta go bud. Hello, Earth to Noah. Get in your seat. Okay, here goes 5-4-3..." Before Sam counted to 1 Noah had jumped over the armrest and into his booster seat with a huge grin on his face. It was always a close countdown. He was very pleased with himself. Jonah was giggling too, with amusement. Sam was being stern but he was equally amused.

After Sam had fixed Noah into his seat he turned over his right shoulder to make sure there were no cars coming around the bend as he approached the driver-side door. The last thing he needed was some nut speeding around the corner of this single lane road and taking his door off the hinges, or worse. All was clear so he got in and closed the door behind him. He affixed his own seatbelt to set a good example for the boys. He started the engine.

"You guys ready to go see Mommy?"

"Mommy, Mommy!" they chanted with excitement in anticipation of seeing their Mom after a long day. Equally important to them was the pride they took in reminding Sam who was still their #1, Mommy.

Sam engaged his left turn signal and looked in the rearview mirror. The setting sun was reflecting strongly, almost blindingly, in the rearview mirror, causing Sam to squint instinctively. This instantly reminded him about how severe his headache really was. This did not help at all. All seemed clear as Sam quickly pulled out of his parking spot and headed for the comfort of home. What Sam failed to see in the convergence of the Sun, his headache, and his blind spot was the pick up truck racing around the corner in his lane. The truck had no time to stop as Sam pulled directly in front of it. Sam never saw it coming before the impact and before he lost consciousness.

Chapter 3

Laura was just finishing up a legal intake with a client in her office. She sat across the desk from this male litigant listening attentively to his story. Being an experienced attorney she had heard so many stories over the years. Many were very similar to each other. However, in some instances the facts were a little varied. Such was the case with Robert Maniakis, a very wealthy, long-time client of the firm.

Normally people seeking representation in defense of a divorce proceeding run the gamut of human emotions from shocked to saddened to furious. This wasn't the case with Maniakis, a distinguished man in his mid-Sixties. He was rather elated at the prospect of moving on with his life. His wife, his 3rd wife that is, of only a few years had served him with divorce papers at his exclusive North Shore Golf Club in an attempt to embarrass him among his contemporaries. He was incapable, however, of such an emotion. To him, everything was business. A wife that didn't want to be with him was no concern other than what it would cost. That is why he kept Laura's prestigious law firm on retainer.

Maniakis had made an appointment with Laura to drop off the divorce papers he was served with together with the pre-nuptial agreement her firm had drafted before the marriage and, of course, the sizable retainer check. Despite the circumstances Robert liked the fact that this "misfortune" gave him a chance to see and talk with Laura again. In a purely platonic way he enjoyed Laura's company and conversation.

As she was concluding the intake session her administrative assistant poked her head into Laura's private office.

"Ms. Job. Sorry to bother you, but there is a call on line 1 for you."

"I told you to hold my calls Mina," she said sternly. With clients paying the kind of hourly fees her firm was charging she didn't appreciate them feeling that her full attention was not focused on them. It just wasn't professional.

"Ms. Job. I apologize, but I think you should take this one. It's about the twins."

At this point Robert Maniakis got up and headed for the door.

"Laura, it's totally fine. I've wasted enough of your valuable time. We are all set for now. Take your call. Call me when the Legal Answer is ready for me to sign."

Laura's whole demeanor changed when she heard the call was about the twins. It was after 6:00PM and she figured Sam had forgotten to pick the twins up from daycare. It was unlike him. He must have gotten distracted or fallen asleep. She was more annoyed than concerned. She picked up the blinking line.

"This is Laura Job. How can I help you?"

"Mrs. Job. This is Police Officer Sheeran of the 8th Precinct. I am sorry to call you like this, but I have some bad news...."

Chapter 4

Sammy Job sat on his bed texting his friend Anna. He and Anna had become quite close over the course of the new school year. This afternoon ritual of texting was a great cure for the loneliness he felt from being home alone every day after school. Sammy had a great affinity for Anna and he thought she did for him; however, he wasn't quite sure if they were boyfriend and girlfriend. Nothing physical had ever happened between them and although he thought about it a lot he never had the courage to initiate the subject. He actually secretly feared ruining what they had. He thought if she rejected his advances that their very special relationship might be damaged forever. He couldn't stand that.

As Sammy looked at the clock on his dresser he realized that they had been texting longer than usual and he hadn't even started his homework yet. He needed to do something before his Dad got home and started the interrogation.

"I gotta go sunshine ttyl," he signed off.

"Night handsome. See you in homeroom."

He opened his Science workbook and started to read about the exciting life cycle of the American mealworm when he noticed that it was later than normal for the rest of his family to start arriving home. When they did arrive it would quickly go from eerily silent to unsettlingly noisy. He thought to himself that he should enjoy it while it lasted.

Sammy did love his brothers. They were sweet and funny and they loved to spend time with their older brother. They were the two people on Earth that no matter what anyone else thought considered Sammy Job cool. They were always good for Sammy's ego for that reason. He loved making them laugh with his silly faces and ridiculous antics. He always got a charge out of them.

But being an older brother to two four year old twins had its challenges though. They always wanted his attention. When they were around and awake, he had no privacy whatsoever. They were always going through his stuff.

"*What is that?*" was a favorite question.

They were always begging to play his video games. Often his attempts at some privacy and peace from Noah and Jonah led to screaming, crying fits, which ultimately caused him some sort of parental trouble. This was a battle he knew he couldn't win. The first rule of being a big brother is that when you fight with little brothers you will always lose.

As for his parents, he got along with them fine for the most part. Things changed a lot after the babies came and even more after his Mom went back to work. Part of it was he was older and more was expected of him. Part of his angst was that he just wasn't the center of his parents' universe anymore. While he didn't recognize that it was a huge issue for him it really was. He loved the years of his parents doting on him, especially with his mother to see him off to school every morning and to be home every day when he got home. He had some resentment over the changes, but it was always tempered by the guilt he felt over the fact that he knew he was being selfish.

Now life had changed a lot. At first he loved the solitude of coming home after school and having the whole house to himself. There was no one home to bother him. No one to tell him what to do. He still relished it; however, he was surprised that he quickly became aware of his isolation and loneliness during the four to six hours he was alone every weekday after school. Part of him looked forward to the chaos and insanity of his family's storming of the castle every evening.

It was his loneliness, as well as his attraction, that fostered his daily texting ritual with Anna. She too had younger siblings and working parents and she understood exactly what he was dealing with. More importantly, he could tell her anything. Things he never shared with anyone he shared with Anna. She never betrayed his trust and she never made him feel foolish. Of all things she was a great friend first and foremost.

Now, as he sprawled out on his bed, completing his Science assignment and thinking about what to work on next he was starting to wonder if he had forgotten about some after school-after work commitment his parents and the twins had today that he was told about but had forgotten. Well, whatever it was they would be home eventually. He wondered how long till dinner and what they were having. He was getting really hungry. Maybe a snack would hold him over.

As he started to outline his English research paper he heard the strong knock at the front door. He ignored it. Usually, when his parents weren't home it was The Jehovah's Witnesses, or some solicitor looking for a donation that he, of course, didn't have. It was always awkward, never productive, and he didn't want to be bothered. His new technique was just to pretend no one was home. They would eventually give up and leave. It worked every time.

The knock this time persisted and, in fact, got even louder. He went to the bathroom window. From this vantage point he had a clear view of the front of his house. He saw a Nassau County Police Car parked in front of his house.

"*What the fuck?*" he said to himself.

He started to think quickly over the last several weeks' activities. Did he do something to warrant getting arrested? He didn't think so. In fact, he was sure that he was safe. He didn't do anything arrest worthy. That was all he needed to tell his Mom.

While he thought it wasn't anything he needed to be concerned about he figured he should answer it. They weren't going away. He walked briskly down the stairs to the front door. He unlatched the door as he took a deep breath. Standing in front of him were two uniformed officers with very serious looks on their faces.

Chapter 5

Three Months Later

Sam Job lay in his hospital bed with his eyes closed. He was unsure whether he was awake or asleep. While his eyes were closed and his mouth was dry he could hear the sound of beeping and the low volume of a television in the background. He must have fallen asleep with the television on again. He hated waking up to the sound and ambient light of the TV. He always forgot to set the sleep timer. While Sam didn't need a lot of sleep, he loved a few hours of complete and undisturbed shuteye.

He could feel the faint warmth of the sun's rays on his cheeks. He must have overslept for work. He was always up and about by the time the sun rose. Why didn't Laura wake him up? Now he could hear Laura whispering. Was she talking to him?

"Please get the doctor. He is starting to move."

"Right away Mrs. Job. I will see who is on call," a female voice responded. Who was Laura speaking to? And why was she in their bedroom?

He began to open his eyes and he was overcome by the brightness. He closed them immediately.

"What is wrong with the lights in here? Laura? What time is it? Why did you let me sleep so long?"

"Babe, it's me. Stay calm. We are not home. You are in the hospital."

"The hospital? For what?"

"Babe, just relax. The doctor will be here soon. He will explain everything."

The doctors had told Laura that if Sam regained consciousness that he might have some memory loss due to the brain swelling. Head trauma patients often experience short-term or long-term memory loss from the impact. Sometimes the memory loss is permanent. The fact is that it was a miracle that Sam did not die in the accident. Another miracle was that his injuries did not appear to make him a quadriplegic or a paraplegic. The doctors said if he regained consciousness he would need extensive rehabilitation, but he should be able to walk again. As for the memory loss there was no way to tell. The possibility existed that he might not even remember Laura or Sam or anyone upon his awakening. In fact, he might not ever remember them.

The doctors warned Laura that no matter what occurred that he would need to be oriented slowly. One day at a time. Information would need to be filtered to him and his ability to process it would determine how much or how little they should say. It was a case-by-case basis. No two head trauma patients have the same experience. The one thing that was for certain was that the dissemination of too much information too soon could set back Sam's recovery significantly.

"I'd better call my office. They are gonna be pissed," he said.

"Sam, it's okay. Everyone knows you are here. They are fine. Don't worry about that."

"When can I go home?"

He tried to sit up, but he didn't have the strength. Despite physical therapy his body had atrophied considerably over the course of the ninety days he was in the hospital. He had lost almost fifty pounds during the course of his stay leaving his tall, broad frame at under 170lbs. He was very weak.

At that moment Dr. Goldberg walked in and put his hand gently on Laura's back.

"Good morning Laura. Good morning Sam."

"Dr. Goldberg?"

Sam had never seen this man before, but he knew instantly who he was. He didn't know how but he was familiar with this doctor. He felt as if they knew each other very well. Polaroiding is the unofficial medical term for it. It involves the ability of a patient's senses to make out the images of people they are in contact with in a trauma situation even if they are not consciously aware of it. Once the patient comes out of their comatose state they will often have recognition of people that have been their caregivers during their infirmity, even though they were seemingly not conscious at the time of contact. Veritable strangers become instantly recognizable to the patient, creating a dichotomy between comfort and confusion.

"Sam, do you know where you are?"

"I am in the hospital? Did I have a heart attack? How long have I been here?"

Dr. Goldberg intentionally avoided the second part of the question.

"No Sam, not a heart attack. You were in an accident. Do you remember anything?"

"Accident? No? What kind of accident? How long have I been here?"

"It was a car accident."

"Really? Was it bad? How is my car? How long have I been here?"

"Sam, you have been here awhile. You need your rest. I think this is enough for now. Why don't you relax and we can talk later."

Sam was starting to get agitated by the lack of response to his question about how long he was at the hospital. He couldn't understand why the Doctor was doing all the talking while Laura stood by silently. That was very unlike her.

"Dr. Goldberg, I appreciate the concern, but I am a big boy. I can handle the truth. I just want some straight answers. First, how long have I been in the hospital? I deserve to know."

Dr. Goldberg, seeing that Sam was getting more agitated not knowing than knowing decided to filter some information about his accident to him slowly.

"You have been here exactly ninety-five days."

"Ninety-five days? Are you kidding me? How bad was the accident?"

"Sam, it was a very bad accident. You were taken by ambulance and admitted through the Emergency Room. You sustained head trauma, a punctured lung, and numerous broken bones. You will, in time and with therapy, make a complete recovery. You are a very lucky man."

"Laura, three months? Oh my goodness. How are you doing?"

"I am fine Sam. Worried about you, but I am fine. You need to rest. One step at a time."

"How is Sammy?"

"Sammy is Sammy. He is okay. He is concerned about his Dad, but he will be okay."

"And my babies? How are the twins?"

With that question Laura grew silent. She was caught a little off guard. She was trying not to cry. She didn't want to, simply, turn and run out of the room, although that was her initial reaction to the question. She really didn't know what to say and she didn't expect to have this reaction. She was almost hoping Dr. Goldberg would throw her a life preserver by stepping in, but she had no such luck. He stood by quietly offering no response. She needed to say something to respond to Sam's question.

"Sam, you need to rest."

"How are the boys? Jonah? Noah? Are they okay? Were they in the accident? Is that what you are hiding from me? Are they hurt? Laura? What is going on?"

Chapter 6

It became quickly apparent to Laura that Sam did not know anything. He seemed to have no recollection of the events of that tragic day or what followed. He didn't even know where he was or why he was there. She was unsure of how she was going to deal with telling him when she wasn't even able to deal with it herself.

Laura raced from her office to the daycare building as soon as the Precinct had contacted her that day. She was in such a hurry that she didn't even take her purse or her cell phone. She grabbed her car keys and jumped in her Dodge Journey and headed for the kids' daycare. She was visibly shaking as she approached the scene. She never should have driven herself. She was not completely in control of her own faculties.

As she approached the accident scene the road was closed and police barricades were mounted everywhere. Traffic was at a complete standstill. She parked on one of the side roads and began running alongside the cars that were lined bumper to bumper on the main road awaiting detour directions from the police. She could see car parts and broken glass all over the road and sidewalk. As she got closer and closer there were more and more of them on the street and sidewalk. Debris was everywhere. She took off her high heel shoes and left them on the road as she tried, desperately, to get to the scene as fast as her legs would take her. She needed to see her babies. She needed to know they were not hurt.

As she gained full visibility of the accident she couldn't even make out what the remnants of any discernible motor vehicles were. She couldn't identify any vehicles and she didn't even know how many were involved in the accident. There was no way to tell. There were just smoking parts and broken glass and tires strewn about. Police, Fire department personnel, and E.M.T's abounded as far as the eye could see. There was a plethora of flashing lights in various colors and sequences emanating from the emergency service vehicles. A large area surrounding the accident had been cordoned off with police tape.

She approached the yellow tape and began to cross the barrier as a uniformed police officer got physically between her and the wreckage and stopped her.

"Ma'am, this is restricted area."

"My babies," she screamed and tried to push past the officer.

Just then Officer Sheeran observed what was going on and quickly made his way to assist. He knew right away that this was Laura Job. He had been anticipating her arrival. As many times as he had dealt with similar situations over the years it never got easier. People in pain was part of the job, but it a part that Sheeran had never adjusted to. He was a husband and a father. He wasn't just a police officer. He was a human being, and a good human being at that.

"Mrs. Job. Officer Sheeran. I know you are upset, but please calm down so we can tend to what we need to."

"Where are my babies? What have you done with them?"

A female officer came to assist. The officers understood completely and they didn't want to use too much force to restrain her, but this was no place for Laura Job to be. The wreckage was too bad. The scene was too grizzly. They needed to protect her from herself. The female officer spoke to her as she helped to create a human barrier between Laura and the wreckage.

"Mrs. Job let's get your shoes. You are going to get cut. Come on, let's walk and get some air."

Ignoring the female officer, she continued to try to push forward.

"I want to see my boys. What have you done with them?"

It was then that Laura looking over the conjoined shoulders of the restraining officers saw the yellow-orange license plate of her husband's car tattered, bent, and lying on the street. Lying next to it was her son Noah's favorite toy, his 11-inch, talking Spider-Man action figure, resting on the street as if it had been gently placed there instead of being thrust from a vehicle upon impact. Upon seeing it Laura lost whatever composure she had left. She pressed harder to get passed the officers who tried desperately to hold her back without hurting her. She started screaming louder and louder and began crying uncontrollably until she finally just collapsed in the arms of the police officers.

Laura's body went limp and she made her way to her knees, on the ground, her chest heaving and sobbing. She was gasping uncontrollably. She was trying not to pass out. She knew now. She knew for certain. She knew then that despite her hopes to the contrary, that her baby boys had been killed in this horrific accident.

Chapter 7

As Sam moved the top half of his electric bed to an upright position Laura dragged a heavy, wooden, hospital chair alongside of him. She understood that she needed to have this conversation with Sam, but she was also sensitive to the condition he was in. He was becoming increasingly persistent in his request for information about his sons. But how much could he handle? What would be too much too soon? Laura really had no idea, but she knew Sam for a long time. She would proceed carefully and stop when she felt it was time. She hoped she would sense when enough was enough.

"Sam, are you sure you are ready to talk about this?"

"Yes. I need to understand what happened? Just tell me where my boys are. Are they okay, Laura?"

"Sam, they're gone."

"Gone. What do you mean gone?"

"Sam, they didn't make it. I know it's hard but they didn't survive the accident."

She hated saying it. It hurt her to the core to say the words. It killed her to tell him that. While he didn't seem to remember anything about the accident, he certainly, remembered the love of his boys. Ironically, and in an almost cruel twist of fate, he remembered everyone and everything leading up to the accident. He knew very well who Jonah and Noah were and what they meant to him.

"How is that possible?" he said putting his hand to cover his open mouth. He then began sobbing and shaking. He was,

clearly, in pain, and, clearly, still very weak from the accident and subsequent coma. Laura took his other hand in hers and bowed her head to touch it. She held her forehead to his hand for quite some time while he just sobbed. She, strangely, couldn't bring herself to hug him. She couldn't embrace him. She wasn't sure why, but she couldn't. It wasn't him. She knew it was an accident. She didn't blame him, at least not knowingly. She wasn't angry with him, for certain. In fact, she pitied him. She just felt dead inside.

After some time Sam regained his composure a little.

"Please tell me what happened. I need to understand."

"Maybe this isn't the right time. You have heard enough."

"Laura," his voice cracking. *"I want to hear this."*

"OK."

Laura then slowly and with as little horrific detail as possible began to recount the events of the day that changed their lives forever. She described for Sam the details of her phone call from the police and her arrival at the scene of the accident. She explained to Sam how the boys and the driver of the other vehicle were killed, instantly, on impact. She was told by the Coroner to take comfort in the fact they likely didn't experience any pain whatsoever. This was of little comfort for her. She also didn't know how they could actually tell her that. They didn't really know for sure. She prayed it for the sake of her little men; however, as a lawyer she was a trained skeptic. Part of her felt the authorities created the fiction that the victims felt no pain simply to ease the pain of the surviving family members.

She did not tell Sam about the absolute decimation she witnessed at the scene. She didn't relay to Sam about the abundance of blood and the debris everywhere. She left out about how she gathered the little bloody shoes of her boys off the street or how she had to go the County Morgue to identify the bodies of their two precious, handsome, unidentifiable angels. She left out the details about Noah's Spider-Man. This would be more than he could handle.

She told him how brave and strong and mature Sammy was accompanying her to Chapey's Funeral Home to make all the arrangements for the wake and the funeral. She retold how they picked out two matching, small, children's coffins for the boys. Children's coffins are something she never knew existed and never dreamed she would be selecting. She told him how she placed their very favorite toys and photos of the family in the coffins with the boys. The funeral parlor employees were all very kind and patient with her and her occasional breakdowns throughout the process. She told him how much that kindness meant to her and Sammy.

Laura paused. She needed a moment to compose herself. As she was telling Sam the story she couldn't help but relive it. It brought back all the emotions she felt at the time and it was very difficult. She didn't want to lose it. Not here. Not now. Not in front of Sam in his condition. It was such a strange change. Sam was normally the strong one comforting her. Not this time. She drank a sip of water and caught her breath and continued.

She told him how overwhelmed she was by the outpouring of support and love during the days of the wake and memorial service. She told him how people from their families and jobs and schools all came out to pay their respects. She told him how total strangers dropped off food and flowers to their home and the funeral parlor. She told him how beautiful the service was that the Priest conducted at the funeral parlor and how brave and mature Sammy was throughout it all. With Sam gone, while she tried not to lean on Sammy too much, he was a source of stability and comfort for her throughout the process. She was so proud of him. She knew he was suffering too.

She shared with Sam how the Church service and funeral were hard for them, but how beautiful they both were. People spoke about the family. Teachers spoke about the joy of having been exposed to these two little boys, even if only for a short time. Sammy spoke at the service about the love he had for his little brothers. He told some cute and, even, funny stories about things the boys used to do that made him mad. His friend Anna was there, by his side, holding his hand the whole time and giving him strength. She had become his rock. Laura was equally impressed by her maturity.

What Laura didn't choose to share. What she couldn't describe. What Laura was unable to articulate was the absolute and palatable pain she experienced seeing the small coffins containing her young sons lowered into the ground at the cemetery. There were no possible words she could use to describe what she experienced during those moments. The only thing she imagined that could be more painful than burying one child was burying two.

In some ways, on this count, she actually envied Sam. While he missed the chance to say goodbye to the boys due to the infirmity that left him unconscious in his hospital bed, he also missed all the pain and all the sadness that she had experienced, alone throughout the last ninety odd days.

She told Sam how in the days following the services people did check in on her and Sammy. While the visits and the calls were less frequent as the days progressed, people still showed genuine concern and she deeply appreciated it. She understood that other people's lives go on. Everyone had their own issues to deal with and people's lives were busy. Their problems would fade to the sad memory category for others, but her family would relive this pain each and every day for the rest of their lives. She knew she would never be the same.

She needed to focus on Sammy and on Sam and on her career. Those three things, she hoped, would keep her distracted enough not to have to deal with the loss so severely.

She told Sam how she spent some time every day by his side. She monitored his progress and she worked with the doctors on a course of treatment to ensure he didn't get worse. At one point she wasn't sure if he would ever recover. She wasn't sure if she wouldn't have to experience all the loss and pain and ceremony all over again if he didn't make it. She didn't know how she and Sammy would have been able to deal with another visit to Chapey's and another wake and funeral. Then Sam woke up and, at least, in that regards life changed a little for the better.

She told him how his job had placed him on State Disability until he was ready to return to the firm. They were very understanding. She returned part-time to work and tried her best to be at work when she was there, fully engaged and with him every morning and evening.

She never considered herself a religious woman but she prayed for him during this time. She prayed that he would survive. She prayed that he would be there for Sammy. She prayed that he would have the strength to deal with the horrible, terrible thing that happened to their family.

She suddenly realized that her head was still leaning against the top of Sam's hand. She hadn't really been looking at him during the recollection of the events of the past ninety days. When she looked up she saw that he was crying. This time not sobbing or heaving, just crying silently into his hand. He cried like this for almost a half an hour before he nodded off into a sleep. He cried himself to sleep.

Laura quietly and carefully removed his hand from hers and placed it gently on his chest. She slowly pushed back the chair from the bed to allow herself room to get up. Laura then walked quietly to the door. She turned and leaned against the inside of the doorway and looked over at Sam. She wasn't sure what she was feeling. She wasn't sure she could feel anything. She wasn't sure she would ever feel again. The one thing she did know was that she was glad that Sam was awake. This gave her some comfort. She then dimmed the lights, pulled the door carefully closed, and walked down the hall towards the hospital Exit.

Chapter 8

Laura's Dodge pulled slowly into the driveway. The door of the attached garage went up automatically as Laura's vehicle approached. The SUV rolled slowly into the place Sam had marked for it. The vehicle's lights shined brightly against the far wall of the garage. Laura manually closed the garage door behind her with the remote control affixed to her sun visor.

She walked quietly into the kitchen through the attached, interior garage door. The house seemed so quiet. She peered over to the dining room table. Sammy had put the mail neatly in a pile for her. She was about to go through it, but she figured it could wait until morning. She could see the outline of some bills, all probably delinquent at this point, and some oddly shaped, colored envelopes, which were likely sympathy cards. She still received several cards a day. Some of these cards were from people she knew and others were from total strangers who had read their story in the newspaper or heard about it from friends. Many of the most comforting sentiments were from the parents of people that had lost children of their own. She read, cherished, and saved each and every one. She left the mail pile on the table and headed upstairs to her bedroom to call it a night. It had been a very long and painful day. Revisiting the accident and the funeral took its emotional toll on her. She was a strong woman but she had been through so much. As she climbed the stairs, she felt like there were large weights about her ankles making each ascending step harder and harder to navigate.

She stopped in front of the twins' bedroom as she did every night. She placed her hand on the knob and stepped inside after taking a deep breath. So many nights she had worked late and

Sam had put the kids to bed before she got home from work. She would turn the knob and enter in just the very same way. Only on those nights she had a very different purpose. Her purpose was to check on her sleeping boys. To make sure they were sound asleep, covered and safe. She also wanted to get the chance to kiss their soft cheeks and smell their freshly bathed hair before she went to sleep. She could still remember their fresh, clean, youthful smells. On those nights she never worried. She always knew the kids were in good hands with Sam. She knew exactly what she would come home to find. She always counted her blessings for him.

These days were different. She walked into the room as if by some miracle she might find the boys sleeping soundly just as they had been on those nights. She knew that this would not be the case, but she needed to walk through their room, untouched from that fateful day they left for school. She walked to the mantle and picked up a picture of Noah and Jonah sitting next to each other on the front stoop of their house, sitting arm in arm. Jonah with his blonde hair and blue eyes looking serious and Noah with his dark brown hair and matching eyes, making a silly face. She smiled as she brought the photo slowly to her lips and kissed them both ever so gently as she closed her eyes.

Laura then walked across the hall to Sammy's room. She put her ear to the door, not to spy but to see if he sounded awake. She could hear the faint noise of music and she knocked softly. No response. She pushed on the handle and saw Sammy sleeping, fully dressed, on top of his comforter. He had headphones about the crest of his head connected to his iPod. That was the music she could hear, from beyond the room. How he slept with all that noise was a mystery to her, but maybe she was just getting old. She put a thin blanket over him and shut his room light. She didn't kiss him for fear she would startle him and disturb his sleep.

She walked into her large, empty bedroom and shut the door behind her. She thought about the day's events as she got undressed for her shower. She tossed her clothes into the hamper almost without any thought at all. She was deep in personal contemplation of her life and her family's current state of affairs. You could have passed a hand in front of her face and she would have been oblivious.

She tested the shower water temperature with her hand and stepped in. She let the water flow over her body. The warm water felt good on her body. She thought about how no matter how bad things were she always felt better, if only for a short time, under the sprinkle of a warm shower. Maybe she could stay here forever.

She shut the faucets and slid open the sliding doors. She toweled her body and her hair. She slowly got into her pajamas. She brushed and blew dry her long brown hair because she knew that if she didn't it would still be damp when she woke up in the morning.

She pulled back her blankets and crawled into bed. She fluffed the pillows and inched to the center of the bed. For as long as she and Sam were together, he always slept on the left side with her on the right. They never switched. Even on vacation, in hotels, it was the same configuration. He had his designated spot with her on the opposite.

"Was it any wonder that Jonah refused to change booster seat spots with Noah," she thought to herself.

But now after almost a hundred days of being alone in their large bed she began gravitating slowly, marginally, towards the center of the bed. It really was a matter of inches. She couldn't say she was getting used to sleeping alone after all those years of being nestled in Sam's embrace, but it wasn't as painful and isolated as it was during the first days she resumed trying to sleep. In the earliest days being alone in the bed, being alone in the house, were both stark reminders of the permanence of the change their family was experiencing.

Now she was alone in their king sized bed. Her last thought before falling into a sleep state was about the image of Sam as she stood in the doorway of the hospital earlier that night. She loved him. She was glad he was doing better, but she couldn't help but feeling, in some ways, like she was staring at a stranger. She felt like she didn't even know who he was. As she faded, she whispered to herself.

"Lord, please help this family find its way."

Chapter 9

Forty-Five Days Later

Sam sat in the wheelchair with his discharge papers on his lap. He had no idea what time Laura would arrive for him, but he was anxious to get out of the hospital. A sure sign that his physical recovery was complete was his increasing lack of complacency about being in the confines of this institution. He went from barely having the strength to get out of bed to not having the patience to be in it over the course of the last month and a half.

Sam's initial physical therapy consisted of short walks along the halls of his hospital floor with a four legged walker. It was the kind of walker you normally saw senior citizens moving about in with tennis balls on the hind legs to keep them from scraping along the ground. Even this task was difficult, at first.

As the days progressed and he gained strength Sam's therapists introduced increasingly challenging tasks to his workout such as walking freely, walking on the treadmill, and eventually using the stair master. Each day he was able to accomplish a little more. He could visibly see and feel the changes in his lower body and his frail, boney legs as they became more toned and muscular. Each step was less and less labored and less and less painful.

As for his upper body, once his legs were a little stronger the therapists introduced working his upper body on the balance bars. The goal was for him to lift his legs and do "dips" where his arms would hold up the entire weight of his body. At first he was unable to complete any, which was understandable in his weakened condition. As his strength grew he began to be able to accomplish this task with some difficulty. Over time the trainers introduced some small barbells as well as a medicine ball. As his discharge date approached he found the regimen far more readily attainable for him. He found himself able to conduct all the physical tasks assigned to him with ease.

Laura wasn't surprised to hear about Sam's progress. As long as she had known him he always was able to bunker down and focus on accomplishing whatever goals he set for himself. It was one of the things that initially attracted Laura to him. He had a "winner's" mentality. If Sam wanted to walk again and it was a medical possibility there was no one more likely to accomplish the task than Sam Job. He would not quit until he was walking as well as before. This Laura knew for sure.

Sam's rehabilitation was not focused solely on the physical. In order for him to integrate back into society he would need extensive counseling of a social and psychological nature. There are very few people that could experience the loss, trauma, and physical isolation from civilization for five months that Sam had experienced without having the need for personal mental health counseling.

Each day Sam met, in two sessions, with a Social worker and a hospital Psychologist to discuss his progress, his feelings, and his expectations. Some of the discussion was focused on his feelings about the tragedy itself while others about setting reasonable expectations on how to cope with issues once released from the hospital. These coping mechanisms included interpersonal dynamics, family relations, and even his expectations upon eventually returning to the workforce.

Sam made progress in the mental health arena too. He came to a better understanding that it was not his fault. He learned some skills to cope with the guilt and anxiety he felt over revisiting the issue and trying to come to the realization that no matter how many times he tried to contemplate the facts, there was nothing he could do in the present to change what had happened on that day.

For Sam one of the most difficult aspects of his emotional state that his therapy tackled was his feelings about his persistent guilt that he was behind the wheel that day, but had no present recollection of anything, at all, whatsoever, after getting into the elevator of his office building to go pick up the twins. For him, he still had great difficulty processing the reality that so much horror and tragedy could have occurred without him having any knowledge of it.

He couldn't fully process the loss of Jonah and Noah because he never had the opportunity to say good-bye. He had great difficulty encoding that he would never see his little twins again because he couldn't remember the accident. His team of therapists worked tirelessly to provide him with the skills and techniques required to deal with the moment or moments that the reality of the finality of the separation between him and his boys set in. For Sam the wake and the funeral were as real as a television show or motion picture to him. He didn't experience them for himself. He didn't share in the common grief of his family. He didn't fully process through all of these traditional bereavement rituals the permanent separation of the physical bodies of his lost boys here on Earth and the transition of their souls to a better place.

Sam was a detail-oriented person. He was a "Type-A" personality. He always looked to put the pieces of the puzzle together to understand the full story in any aspect of his life. Now this full story included him accidentally taking the life of his beloved children and a total stranger and he felt like he knew nothing.

This aspect of the story was equally unsettling to him. Who was this pickup truck driver? Did he have a family? What would become of them? How much or little should he do to pursue this information, and even to pursue seeking out their family.

This was all a great deal for Sam to handle, but this is what filled his life for the month and half after he regained consciousness. Sam was a smart man and he was also a realist. He understood that this was a process. He understood that even he did not know what he had in store for him once he was discharged. He intended to meet each day one at a time and he pledged to seek the help and support of professionals when he needed to.

Once of the greatest concerns for the doctors was the uncertainty about the loss of memory Sam experienced. While it seemed that his memory of the incident was permanently erased from his consciousness, it was possible that it would return to him in stages, in fragments, or in whole. The consistent goal of the doctors was to create a structure for Sam not to attempt to reconcile all of these recollections on his own if this were to occur. Despite the fact that he did have some knowledge of what occurred from what he heard and read it was not the same thing. Were these recollections to return it was unclear how well equipped Sam would be to weather the storm of emotions those memories might bring. He needed to be prepared to seek guidance at that time.

As Sam sat in his wheelchair thinking about Noah and Jonah he felt a mix of rage, loss, and sadness. He wished he had spent more time with them. He wished he hadn't been so strict with them sometimes. He wished he never went to pick them up on that fateful day. As his fingers curled on the armrest of the wheelchair in an almost maniacal grip he saw Laura cross the threshold of the room.

"You sure you are ready? It's okay if you aren't. I want you to be sure. Another couple of days?"

"No. It is time. I am physically able to take care of myself now and I miss being with you and Sam. I gotta start thinking about work."

"Slow down Sam," she said soothingly. "One step at a time. The doctors said you already have all the discharge paperwork, course of treatment, and prescriptions?"

"Yes, I have everything."

"You have a follow up appointment set and an appointment with the therapist booked?"

"Yes. I have everything in place. Can we go now, please?"

"Okay Sam."

She walked around the back of his chair, kissed him on the top of the head, and lifted the safety latch wheelchair brakes with her right foot releasing the wheels to roll freely. She then turned and positioned Sam towards the hallway and walked towards the elevator. As they passed the nurse's station and the medical personnel they said their goodbyes. Both Sam and Laura made it a point to say thank you to all of them. For both of them five months of daily interaction with the hospital staff drew them very close to these hospital caregivers. The doctors, nurses, CNA's, therapists, physical therapist, candy stripers, and security guards all knew Sam and Laura. They knew their names. They all knew their sad story. They all knew their family and they took exceptional care of both of them in so many ways. They were good, decent, and kind people. While Sam and Laura wouldn't exactly miss them, they would always remember them.

Laura pushed the down button on the elevator and the center light flashed as they waited for its arrival. As the elevator approached and the doors opened Laura and Sam knew these were important steps towards the rest of their lives. For Laura, she tried hard not to let Sam see the tear roll down her left cheek as the elevator doors came to a close.

Chapter 10

Sammy sat on the edge of Anna's bed facing her. His upper body was turned slightly towards her while his feet were planted firmly on the ground. He ran his right hand through her hair as he kissed her softly on the lips. Her eyes were closed, but his open. Her left hand stroked the side of his face as she kissed him back. Sammy opened his mouth and moved his tongue into Anna's mouth. She reciprocated.

Anna had been Sammy's rock throughout the entire tragic ordeal. From the moment the police had knocked on his door his life had changed forever. The sudden loss of his brothers. His father's coma. The chaos and anxiety of the days subsequent to the accident were emotionally unbearable for Sammy to deal with. He wasn't emotionally equipped to deal with all this sadness and pain. His life had been relatively mundane up to this point. He never had any real stress or anxiety aside from the normal childhood angst. His home was safe and secure. His parents were good people, albeit annoying at times. His brothers were his joyful *"pains in the butt"* as he often referred to them. Whether Sammy understood it or not, for him, life was pretty good before that fateful day.

Of all of the difficulties for Sammy in dealing with the death of his baby brothers the hardest thing, by far, that he had to deal with was seeing his Mom suffer so much. He knew that she was trying to keep a brave exterior for him, but he knew her too well. They were too much alike. He knew that as much pain as she was exhibiting on the outside it was just the tip of the iceberg. He knew she was torn apart inside. She was a good Mom. She was involved in all of their lives. Despite working she still found time to make sure each and every one of the men in the house, big and little, were taken care of. He loved his mother's nurturing heart.

Sammy knew it was an accident. He knew his Dad was not a reckless or careless guy. He understood his Dad would never do anything to put anyone of his family in danger. Yet Sammy struggled with anger, resentment, and even hate, at times, for his father over the loss of his siblings and over the dramatic changes that occurred in their family due to the accident. He knew it was wrong to feel this way. He knew it was selfish and horrible to resent a man who did so much for his kids and who must still be suffering so much. He knew his Dad would have died to bring those boys back but still he couldn't even bring himself to visit him in the hospital. All these conflicted thoughts lead Sammy to one overwhelming emotional response; crippling guilt.

Amidst all of Sammy's suffering he found an oasis in the desert of his emotional angst. That oasis was the emergence of his undying friendship with Anna. From being his texting soul mate Anna emerged as a mature, loyal, deeply thoughtful friend. Despite being only six months older than Sammy, in the midst of the crisis, it seemed like they were a generation apart in some ways. She was, herself, a nurturing, and mature caregiver. She reminded him, in a healthy way, of all of the good qualities of his Mom.

Anna was there to help and support his family during this worst of times. She amazed Sammy and even Laura how she unselfishly stepped in to provide whatever assistance she could towards easing the burden of a difficult time. She was by Sammy's side to hug him, to hold his hand, to support him, and to help get him ready for the wake and funeral. She helped his Mom with straightening up the house before and after the cavalry of people that were in and out of their house in the days surrounding the tragedy. She did all of it without seeking praise and while managing to be unobtrusive, discrete, and not overbearing in her assistance.

Through it all they never discussed the evolution of their relationship from friendship to more. Anna had no ulterior motive. She was by Sammy's side because she really cared about him and she really felt his loss. While she didn't know his little brothers well it didn't matter. How could she not feel the suffering of a family that was just robbed of the lives of two babies? More personally, how could she not help and attend to her friend, Sammy. For Anna, this was the essence of what friendship was about. So when Sammy walked her home the night after the funeral and he stood at her front door he started to speak.

"Anna, I don't know how to thank..."

With that she, instinctively, put her index finger on his lips to stop him from speaking and leaned in to kiss his mouth slowly. It was nothing inappropriate. It was nothing scurrilous. It was just a kiss, but they both understood that it was more. It was an escalation and an evolution of their friendship to something more.

Now they sat on her bed in the bedroom of her family's home with the door shut. Had anyone else been home the door would surely have been open. While Anna's family was liberal they still had a policy that forbid boys in her bedroom with the door closed, as well as boys in the house when no one else was home, but here they were.

"Are you sure you want to do this?" Sammy asked. *"We don't have to."*

"I know we don't have to. I want to."

When Anna spoke these words, there was no pressure. It wasn't that she was forcing the issue. She, certainly, wasn't forcing Sammy to do anything he didn't want to. She simply wanted to reassure him that she cared and that she was ready to share something more with him.

For Sammy, he was a virgin, and a little unsure of exactly how to proceed. He didn't want it to be awkward, but he knew from their conversations that Anna was a little more experienced and would guide him along the way.

Guide him she did. She removed her own skirt and underwear, barely lifting herself from her position next to Sammy and without separating her lips from his. Then she moved her hands to his waist to unbutton his jeans. With that gesture Sammy jumped up a little. To say Sammy was just a little nervous would be a huge understatement. He proceeded to unzip his pants and lower them to the floor, revealing his blue and gray striped boxer shorts, making him feel particularly vulnerable despite his comfort with Anna.

Carefully Anna leaned in to resume kissing Sammy and relax him. She was prepared to take it slowly but she did feel exceptionally close to him. Sammy was a kind and decent guy. Since the onset of puberty she never really had a boy that she maintained such a close friendship with. She had some boyfriends in the past, but it was different. None were like Sammy.

Anna moved their position slightly higher on the bed. It was almost like they were ballroom dance partners and she was in the lead. She then lowered herself to a horizontal position guiding Sammy on top of her, their lips still joined.

Sammy was enjoying Anna's warmth and embrace more than anything. He had felt so lonely. He had felt so alone. He had felt so empty. Now he could feel her two hands moved slowly down his back and onto the waistband of his underwear. As Anna lowered his underwear, exposing his flesh against hers, he did not resist. They were both clearly impassioned and excited but this was not an expression of lust, even for these relative novices, it was an expression of love.

"I love you Anna."

"I love you too, baby. Just relax. You are doing great."

Anna, continuing to recognize Sammy's inexperience and slight awkwardness, then guided her hand between his legs and helped him join her for the first time. The union didn't last long, although, for Sammy it was an eternity. He was completely and totally lost in her. Nothing else mattered at this moment. He felt no pain. He felt no guilt. He felt no isolation. He felt no loss. For the first time in almost five months he actually felt alive.

As they regained their breath and their composure Sammy felt like he should say something.

"I am really sorry."

"Sorry! Don't ever say that. Please don't ruin it. I wanted to. I care about you. I wanted to share myself with you. It was wonderful, amazing, fantastic."

True to form Anna always seemed to know the right thing to say to him at just the right time.

"Come lay next to me. We have a little while before we have to get out of here before my parents get home. Let's enjoy it."

Sammy did enjoy it at first. He felt very lucky to have someone so close as Anna by his side. It was, oddly enough, his overwhelming sense of joy and companionship that made him start to feel it as he lay on her bed with her head on his bare chest. He began to think about how great this was and began to consider that he didn't deserve it. He thought about the most powerful and wonderful sensation he had just experienced and began to articulate to himself that it was wrong to indulge himself in this time of pain for his family. He began to think about how great it was to have Anna by his side, but then he began to consider the events that brought them closer.

As Sammy lay next to Anna he could feel himself beginning to become unhinged. His brothers were dead. They would never return. These babies weren't even gone six months and he was having the time of his life. Part of him knew he was being illogical. Part of him knew it wasn't like that at all but he started to become overcome by feelings of guilt and shame. Shame. He started to feel dirty and selfish. He didn't want to cry. He didn't want to make Anna feel bad. She didn't deserve to be hurt now too. He began to consider that he was the worst person on the planet. He began to have horrible thoughts. With that he tried gently but unsuccessfully to move Anna's head from his chest.

"Where are you going?" she asked.

"I just have to use the bathroom."

"Okay, hurry back. We only have a couple of more minutes."

"Sure."

Sammy walked into the bathroom connected to Anna's bedroom. It was pink and very obviously a women's bathroom. He quietly locked the door behind him. He looked around the counter in search of something amidst Anna's curling iron, blow dryer, and other feminine utensils. He then opened the medicine cabinet with single-minded determination.

More than several minutes had passed when Anna started to wonder what was up. Maybe all those nerves got to Sammy's stomach? She got up and tossed her underpants in the hamper. She pulled the skirt up and around her waist. She then walked over the bathroom door and knocked gently.

"Babe?"

She waited, but no response. She knocked again, a little more firmly this time.

"Sammy. It's me. You alright in there?"

Still no response. She wasn't sure why, but she started to feel anxious. She banged a lot harder now.

"Sammy. Open the door. I am worried. Whatever it is we can talk about it."

No noise whatsoever. Anna then felt around the top of the molding surrounding the door. There was a key there for the innumerable times she locked herself out of her own bathroom. Anna quickly fumbled to get the key in the door, calling Sammy's name a little frantically at this point. She heard the lock click to open and she turned the knob and raced into her bathroom. She was horrified by what she found.

Chapter 11

An uncomfortable silence filled the car as Laura and Sam motored towards their house. Several times along the way Laura attempted to mouth the words to engage in some trivial conversation with Sam but she stopped herself each time. She found herself at a complete loss for what to say to this man that she knew for almost thirty years. The man seated next to her was a man that she had built a life with. Sam was her companion and friend for almost three decades. He was the father of her three children. This is the man she had been through so much with together. As she drove to their house together she found herself in the company of a complete and total stranger.

"You okay Sam?"

"Yes, I am fine. I think."

"Do you need to stop anywhere on the way home?"

"No, thank you," he said politely.

His response was followed by a dead and awkward silence between them. She then decided to turn on the radio to fill the void of silence. Fumbling for a radio station while driving seemed to be an easy way to avoid conversation between them. She turned the radio tuner to CBS 880AM. One of a million car commercials played on the radio before returning to the regular news broadcaster.

"The trial of a man who confessed to kidnapping and murdering 6-year-old Etan Patz, the boy whose disappearance sparked a nationwide movement to find missing children 35 years ago, ended in a hung jury Friday after 18 days of deliberations."

Laura leaned over and quickly switched the radio off. Bad idea! There was no need for such stark reality so soon after Sam's release from the hospital. The doctors had limited Sam's initial exposure to television, even as a background accompaniment for fear that graphic news stories about his accident would be too shocking for him to process. There was rarely good news being reported these days.

"Sorry Sam."

"You really never have to apologize to me. Anyway, I am gonna have to get used to the world again at some point."

"Yes, true, but not yet. It's too soon."

Sam appreciated Laura's concern. Hearing the news story about Etan Patz didn't have a dramatic impact on him she thought it would though. It was also a horrific story. He remembered when it had first occurred. He remembered how shocked everyone was and how the story changed, forever, how people in the NYC Metro area dealt with the supervision of their children. This sweet, innocent boy's face became the permanent symbol of how cruel and evil the world could be sometimes.

The problem for Sam was that, for him, certain aspects of his own tragedy were no more real to him than the story of Etan Patz. While he felt the personal grief over the loss of his sons, he felt as removed from the circumstances as he did from this story he read about in the papers. Part of him wished his full memory would return to him so he could begin to fully process all of his feelings about what had occurred and what had followed. He felt like knowing even the worst of details of the tragedy would be easier for him than filling in the blanks from other sources.

Sam could sense Laura's distance. He wasn't sure exactly what it stemmed from. Was it concern over his fragility? Was it anger at him for what he had done to her and Sammy? Was it that she had lost her ability to "feel" the rhythm of the world. Had a numbness set in that might be impossible to break? Sam didn't fully understand what Laura was feeling and he didn't want to barrage her with questions, nor did he have the strength to. He figured he would be as independent as he could so as not to burden her and, hopefully, in time, she would open up to him about what she was feeling and what she needed.

As they turned on the their block they both seemed to breath a sigh of relief. It would be easier, perhaps, if they weren't side by side in the confines of her SUV. As she pulled slowly into the open garage door and shut off the car she looked over at him.

"Welcome home, Sam."

"Thanks Laura."

Laura walked around to the passenger side and opened the door for Sam. He got out slowly placing once foot on the ground at a time. He then shut his own door and headed into the house. He suddenly realized he hadn't been home since he left the house that morning to drive the boys to school. He hesitated. He took a deep breath and then continued his entry into their home, following Laura's lead.

They crossed the threshold into the kitchen and Laura called out to Sammy.

"Sammy? Sammy?"

No response. Weird. He knew she was bringing his Dad home today. Maybe he was asleep.

"Let me run up and see if he is asleep."

"Don't disturb him. He will come down when he's ready. It's probably hard for him to see me."

"He loves you Sam. He was worried about you. He is just a kid. It has been really hard on him, but you would have been so proud of him."

"I am proud of him. He is a good boy. I mean it. He will come around when he is ready. I don't want to force it."

With that Laura hugged him gently. She patted him several times on the right shoulder as she did. These hugs were more reserved for a distant relative or acquaintance than a beloved partner and friend. As she hugged him her cell phone rang. She was surprised to see the caller's name and number appearing on the display. It was Anna. Weird. She answered.

"Hi Anna. Hold on. Slow down. Take it easy. Sweetheart, you are hysterical. I can't understand you."

"What do you mean? When? Oh My God! How? What did the doctors say?"

"Anna, where is he right now? Are you there with him? I need you to calm down. I am on my way. I will be there in twenty minutes tops. I have my cell phone on. If there is any change you call me right away."

"What is going on?" Sam asked as she hung up, not certain who she was talking to or about.

"It's Sammy. He tried to kill himself."

"What? Are you serious? Oh my goodness."

"He is at 1 North Psychiatric Hospital in Syosset. She said he tried to cut his wrists. There was a lot of blood and he passed out but that he will be okay. She said they are holding him on a seventy-two hour hold for a full psychiatric evaluation, but that he is safe."

"Sam, maybe you should stay here. This is too much too soon. You rest."

"No way Laura. I am going with you. He is my son, too, for God's sake."

"I know Sam. I understand. Let's go."

So, no sooner than they entered the home they departed. They got back into her SUV, backed out of the driveway, and drove quickly towards the Psychiatric Hospital housing their beloved son. This time there was no issue of small talk or radio programs. Understandable and palpable silence filled the cabin. They were both singularly focused on one thing and one thing only, making sure they didn't lose another son.

Chapter 12

Laura pulled the Dodge Journey up to the valet attendant's area and rolled down her window.

"Excuse me. Where is 1 North?"

"It is on the first floor through these doors, on the left. Do you want me to park your car for you, Mrs.?" the young man, just barely older than Sammy, asked.

"Yes, please. I am running in. You can give the ticket to my husband."

Laura then placed the car in park and swung open her door. She looked over to Sam.

"Take your time. Meet me inside. I am going in."

"Go ahead. I will be right behind."

She raced through the revolving doors and was out of Sam's visibility. While the valet made his way to the driver side of the car Sam pulled himself out of the passenger seat and planted both feet firmly on the ground. He leaned over to the valet and stuck a $5 bill in his hand.

"Thank you. In the event that the valet station closes before we leave where will the keys be?"

"You are welcome. After 11PM they will be with security. I hope everything is okay with your loved one."

He was a nice kid. He seemed very mature and very sincere.

Sam made his way slowly through the front door and followed the young man's instructions. He arrived at a security guard sitting in front of a secure door marked "1 North". She was a heavyset, African-American woman, around fifty years old, wearing a white uniform shirt with matching navy slacks. As he approached her station she looked up at him from her seat.

"I am Sam Job. My son Sammy was admitted here earlier. Can I see him?"

"Yes, sir. I just need to see some identification."

Sam thought to himself for a moment and realized he didn't have a clue where his wallet was. He had never even asked about personal belongings. He didn't need any ID or money in the hospital. He never considered needing his identification so close to being discharged from the hospital.

"I don't have anything on me. I just got out of the hospital. My wife checked in already."

The guard hesitated and thought about it for a moment. Hospital rules required her to verify visitor's ID before letting any person past the ward entrance. She got up and leaned over the desk and spoke softly.

"It's okay Mr. Job. I know who you are. I saw your story on the news. I am so sorry about the loss of your boys. Your wife mentioned you were following behind her. Go on in. We are not gonna lose this one too. Don't you worry."

She was speaking very gently and softly the whole time. Despite all the sadness he had been experiencing he began to become starkly aware of the compassion he was being shown by total strangers. Maybe he was just more aware of it now than before the accident. He wasn't sure. This security guard was, clearly, going above and beyond her call of duty to be kind to him. She pressed the buzzer and opened the door to the Psychiatric ward of the hospital. Sam thanked her and walked into the waiting area touching her arm slightly in appreciation as he passed.

The first thing that Sam saw was Laura face to face with a young woman he assumed to be Anna. Laura was hugging her. She was holding her closely. The girl was obviously sobbing into Laura's shoulder as Laura stroked her hair.

"It's okay sweetie. It's not your fault. Sammy loves you. He is going to be fine. The doctor told me so. I just spoke to him. He doesn't even need surgery."

Anna continued to sob, but she seemed to calm slightly with Laura's encouraging words and warm touch.

"Listen Anna. I know Sammy. He has dealt with all this as well as he has because of your friendship. It is just a lot for him to handle. I should have had him in therapy sooner. It could have been so much worse."

"This was classic Laura," Sam thought to himself. Even in a crisis, she managed to find a way to put her feelings aside and comfort others. She was someone very special. As he was watching Laura and Anna a white-haired, Asian looking man in a short, white lab coat quietly approached them from beyond a locked set of double doors. He appeared to be a doctor.

"Mr. & Mrs. Job?"

"Yes. That's us."

"I am Dr. Park. I am the Supervising Doctor here. Can we talk privately?"

He was referring to Anna's presence. For confidentiality reasons he couldn't speak in front of her as she was not a spouse or a blood relative. His demeanor was very calm and professional.

"Anna, honey. Why don't you give us some time to speak with the doctor. Go sit and relax, or get yourself a cup of coffee and once we are finished with him we can talk more about Sammy."

"Will I be able to see him?" Anna asked.

"Sure. As soon as the doctors give us permission."

Anna leaned back in and hugged Laura. The two separated slowly with Anna holding onto Laura's left hand as she did, almost struggling to let go. Anna then walked slowly down the hall to the seating area for family and friends with her head bowed.

"Hello, Dr. Park. How is Sammy?" Laura asked as she and Sam moved in closer to form a semi-circle around the doctor.

"The good news is that your son is going to be alright. The cuts were deep, but he didn't manage to sever anything that would cause real harm. He didn't need surgery on his wrists. He is bandaged and he will heal."

Both Sam and Laura began to tear up as the doctor was talking.

"As for his mental state it is not good. I understand he recently lost two brothers in an accident?"

"Yes, doctor, and his Dad was in the hospital recovering from the accident for the last six months."

"Well, it seems that all of the pressure was a little more than he could handle. The fact that he didn't do serious harm to himself doesn't mean that he didn't intend to. I don't think this was a cry for help. I think it was a legitimate suicide attempt. Being a 'normal' teenager is hard enough, but the added stress got to him."

"So what now?"

"We are mandated to hold him for seventy-two hours. He is a minor. The decision on what happens next is yours? I suggest he stay here indefinitely until we get him a little better adjusted."

"Indefinitely?" they said in unison.

"Don't be alarmed. What that simply means is without an exact discharge date at the time of admission. I expect it will be a few weeks at most. He is a smart boy. He just needs some support and some therapy and to build some coping mechanisms."

"Okay, of course doctor. Whatever course of treatment you suggest we will support. We just want him to get better."

"He will need to have an outpatient Psychiatrist to take over his treatment upon his discharge. We will also evaluate the need for short term medication."

"Can we see him?"

"Yes. They are getting him settled in a room and then if you want you may see him. I want you to know that he is in good hands and I expect he will make a full recovery. He doesn't seem to have any underlying mental health issues that would complicate treatment. Listen, he has been through a trauma. This is something we can manage in time and with care. You may wish to have the rest of the family in therapy, too."

"Thank you doctor. We will be in the waiting area. Will they let us know when we can see him?"

"Yes. And I am so sorry about the loss of your boys."

Dr. Park, having finished this briefing then retreated to the corridor beyond the double doors separating the treatment area from the waiting room.

Laura looked somewhat relieved. It wasn't a shock that Sammy might be overcome by all that had happened to their family. This would be a good place for him to rest and get some help that Laura and Sam were, clearly, unable to provide. It is not that Sam and Laura were unwilling to help him. It was simply above their pay grade. They had so many issues of their own surrounding the loss that they were ill equipped to be mental health caregivers for Sammy at the apex of his anxiety.

"Sam. Why don't you sit here and wait for the doctor. I am going to go talk to Anna and fill her in on what the doctor said."

Laura turned and walked towards Anna in the seating area. She sat next to Anna, put her hand on her leg, and started to fill her in on what was going on with Sammy.

Sam sat in an empty chair, in an isolated overflow waiting area, down the hall from where the ladies were sitting. He was well out of the range to hear the exact conversation between them but he could see them. He was watching Laura from the distance. He was really impressed by her compassion, her leadership, and her humanity in this crisis. She was grace under pressure.

He thought about Sammy. A teenage boy shouldn't have to endure what Sammy was dealing with. Sam's first recollection of the loss was his grandparents' death when he was a teenager but that was different. They were elderly and, while it is never easy to lose a loved one, you come to expect death as people age. It is part of the natural cycle of life. The death of babies is not natural. It is not normal. It goes against the natural order of things. It is a wonder Sammy didn't crack sooner.

"Things will be different now," Sam thought.

Now that he was home, he would make an effort to show Sammy how proud they both were of him. He would show Sammy how much he meant to the family and how lucky his brothers were to have such a great older brother. He would show Sammy how much they loved him. How much he loved him. He would make up for the time he was away. He would, they would, heal as a family.

Sam was so deep in thought about Sammy that he didn't notice Laura approach. She had walked right next to him and was now looking directly down at him.

"*Hey,*" she said.

"*Hey.*"

"*Can we talk Sam?*"

Chapter 13

Sam wasn't exactly sure why Laura's question was posed with such formality. He was still having great difficulty understanding exactly what Laura was thinking. It was a dramatic change from what he was used to. After so much time together he and Laura almost always knew where the other one was coming from even when they disagreed. He often could finish her sentence before she finished uttering it and vice-versa. Not now, though. He had no idea what was on her mind. He, too, felt estranged in the relationship.

"Of course. Talk to me."

Laura took a deep breath and joined her hands together, palms facing each other in a prayer like position as she slowly sat in the chair next to Sam's.

"How's Anna?" he inquired.

"Okay, I think. She will be better when she sees Sammy. She blames herself. She is a good girl."

"What's up Laura?"

She paused. She said nothing for almost thirty seconds before beginning to speak.

"Sam. You know I love you?"

"Of course."

"Good. I do love you. I have loved you since the first moment I met you. Each milestone in our life has been so special. When you asked me out. When you proposed. The day we got married.

The birth of each of the boys. Every single moment of it all I have loved you with all my heart."

While Laura was busy professing her love for Sam he couldn't help but feel like this wasn't simply an attestation of her affection for him. While he was humbled by the words she was speaking, he felt unease about his uncertainty over what was about to follow. He knew it wasn't merely a summary of her love for him. There had to be more on the horizon.

"While you were in that hospital, I prayed every night for your recovery. Sammy and I couldn't stomach the thought of losing you."

"Well, you didn't. I am here."

"I know Sam and I am so happy for you. I know it has been hard for you on so many levels. I understand that your physical recovery is just the beginning. I want you to know I will be here for you to help you."

"I know that."

He placed his hand gently on her face, which she judiciously but noticeably removed.

"Sam, please let me finish..."

"Sam, no matter what you may think I don't blame you for what happened. I never have. Not for one second since this all happened. I know it was an accident. I know you would never, ever, ever do anything to harm Jonah or Noah or Sammy or me."

Sam found himself becoming very emotional hearing Laura express these sentiments. While he wasn't certain it was true, it meant a lot to hear her express it. Regardless of what she said they all knew that, but for his actions they wouldn't be sitting in a psychiatric hospital with Sammy, mourning the loss of his brothers. He became increasingly emotional, but he used all of his willpower to hold back from breaking down. He feared that if he lost his composure that Laura would not finish what she was trying to tell him. This is what he felt she was trying to express for the two months since he awoke and finally got the courage to articulate. He didn't want to disrupt her now.

"Sam, I always pictured that we would grow old together. I always thought about you and I, retired, traveling to exotic locations and drinking Raki on the beach somewhere as the sun went down."

"Me, too"

"and maybe someday that is how this will all end up." Laura paused.

"Sam, I hope you know I would never do anything to hurt you. Never. I will always be there for you. You are now and always have been my one, true love."

"But..." he interrupted.

Sam wasn't being rude or harsh. He was, simply, following the conversation and in Laura's pause what he was thinking got muttered out loud.

"But... I think we need some time apart."

"Time apart?"

"Yes, Sam. I know this is hard. I am sorry for the timing, but I can't be with you right now. I don't know how to express it Sam, but everything has changed now. I feel empty and alone and in so much pain every day. Every minute it is so hard not to just crawl into bed, go under the covers and wait for this nightmare to end. But it isn't a nightmare. It is our lives. Sam, right now I am no good for you. I am no good for myself. I am no good for

nobody. I need to get myself together and focus on getting Sammy right. That is what I need to devote my life too. I, we, can't lose that boy. He has so much life to live. His life shouldn't be over at sixteen because this happened."

"Laura, I know that. We are together on this. I will help you with Sammy. We can all go to therapy. We can try to find a way to cope with this."

"I can't Sam. Not right now. Please don't make this harder than it is. I do love you. It isn't about you at all and for that I am even more sorry. Sam, I am just scared. I have thought about it since the moment you opened your eyes. I, probably, never would have said anything for a while if it weren't for this issue with Sammy. I need to do this now Sam."

"Laura. I really am not sure what to say. You know I love you more than anything in the world. I would give anything to bring Jonah and Noah back. If I could have traded my life for theirs, I would do it in a heartbeat. I know you are in pain. I also see how uncomfortable you are around me. It makes me sad. Not sad for me. Sad for you. You don't deserve this."

"Sam it isn't about deserve. We didn't deserve any of this. Jonah and Noah didn't deserve any of this. Sammy doesn't deserve any of this, but here we are."

"Sam, I am not going anywhere. I will help you any way I can but I just need some physical separation for the time being. When, if, things turn around and you still want to give it a chance I will be here waiting. I just need you to do this for me. I need us to walk out of here today knowing that we are both clear on this. I am sorry Sam."

Sam took a deep breath. His emotions fluctuated from panic to sadness to understanding. He knew Laura was in pain. He knew she would never hurt him intentionally. That just wasn't Laura. He knew that if she said this is what she needed, then this is what she needed. What choice did he have? He loved her. He loved her so much that as unbearable as the thought was of being without her was, it was nothing compared to knowing she was in pain being together with him. While he honestly didn't fully understand, **love isn't always about understanding it is about trusting**. He knew he needed to trust that Laura knew what she needed and he needed to honor her no matter how painful it was.

Sam stood up slowly. Slowly, mostly, because he couldn't stand up any other way. His body was too weak. He placed both of his hands gently on either side of Laura's head. He bent over and kissed her ever so softly on the top of her head. His nose filled with the familiar odor of Laura. Not her shampoo. Not her perfume. His nostrils filled up with the familiar odor that was all hers and hers alone. It provided immediate comfort and tranquility for Sam. It was the most calm and familiar moment he had felt since his awakening. He didn't know what the future held, but he knew he loved her and he knew he must comply with her wishes.

"Okay, my sweet. Whatever you need me to do is fine. I will be waiting for you when you are ready. Just focus on Sammy and we will figure it all out over time."

She looked him directly in the eyes. She realized it was, perhaps the first time she had done so since the day he left their house to drive the twins. She looked deeply, thankfully into his eyes with a sense of relief.

"Thank you Sam Job. Don't forget I love you."

Sam then felt the need to take a walk and stretch his legs while waiting for them to see Sammy. He looked at Laura and changed the subject from the discussion of their relationship.

"I am gonna stretch my legs. I will stay on this floor. I should only be a few minutes. If I am not back by the time we can see Sammy can you come get me?"

"Sure Sam. I think we still have some time. Just be careful. Don't do too much."

Sam turned his back slowly from Laura and turned the corner of the hospital floor with no real destination in mind.

Chapter 14

As Sam turned the hospital corner he became deeply lost in thought. He began to run through a montage of his entire life. It played like a high-speed video in his mind. He considered the earliest days of his childhood that he could remember through and including the day of the accident.

"What have I done to bring this blight upon my family?" he asked himself.

When Sam asked this question it wasn't really rhetorical. He was actually on a mental and emotional quest to search the database that was his memory for some answers as to what he could have done to bring this tragedy down upon himself and his family. He sincerely couldn't think of anything. Nothing jumped out at him, big or small. He had always tried to live a good and honorable life. He had never committed any major sin that came to mind. He never cheated. He never stole. He was honest. He strove to be the best husband, the best father, the best son, the best citizen he could be. The truth is that his life, his whole life before the accident, was blessed. Not extraordinary, but blessed.

Sam thought about his relationship with God. Sam always considered himself to be a religious person. He was more religious than many, for certain. He was more religious than Laura. More overtly, religious that is. He was more comfortable with the construct of organized religion than Laura. Perhaps, he was a little less skeptical than Laura, by nature, not to say that he was any more devoted to God than she was. But what did any of that mean? He just didn't know.

He attended Church occasionally. Not weekly, but occasionally. He prayed often. Most importantly, at least he thought most importantly, he lived a good and Godly life. He never, intentionally, harmed anyone in his entire life.

While Sam Job never measured or analyzed the tragedies of others as being the result of the wrath of an angry God, or the result of having lived a bad life he was now asking these questions about his own tragedy. He was now looking for the first time for the causal link between his behavior, between his life, between his actions, between his thoughts, and his suffering.

Maybe he didn't attend Church enough. Maybe he wasn't kind enough. Maybe he didn't pray enough. Maybe he wasn't as kind and decent as he purported to be. He was far from perfect in all areas of his life. He understood that. Maybe he made too many excuses for his own shortcomings. But did those things really warrant what had happened to his family? Did they warrant the loss of two lives? Did they warrant the death of babies? Did they warrant the suffering of Sammy and Laura? He couldn't reconcile any of it.

As Sam continued to walk, he looked up at the ceiling and muttered to himself.

"What have I done to make you so angry?"

Chapter 15

Sam walked for a little while more until he came upon a sign that read "Hospital Chapel". He thought to himself that this was, perhaps, a good time to seek comfort in the bosom of the Church. He slowly turned the knob and walked in quietly so as not to disturb anyone who was deep in prayer. He surveyed the room. It was a small, clean chamber. There was a short, center aisle with traditional looking wooden pews on either side leading to a front table that had the appearance of a makeshift alter. Each row appeared to have a number of hard covered, black bibles on them for reading and attached kneelers for prayer. The walls were blank. There appeared to be no statutory present. There was no visible Iconography. Just a small, plain, wooden cross mounted above the center table.

To his surprise the Chapel was empty but for an elderly gentleman who appeared to be returning the bibles to the racks in front of each of the pews. The man looked about eighty years old. He was balding. He had thick glasses with a gray mustache and neatly trimmed, goatee. Sam assumed he must be the Hospital Chaplain.

"Come in my son. Don't let me stop you. I am just straightening up."

"Thank you Father." Sam said politely. *"I was just hoping to pray for a bit."*

"Well you have come to the right place. Some people think secular hospitals should do away with Chapels. If they sat in here for an average day I think they would reconsider."

Sam moved to one of the pews. He knelt before entering and crossed himself as he sat down not really sure whether to kneel and pray or read the Bible. He found himself observing the Chaplain going about his work.

"Do you want to talk about it son?"

"I don't want to disturb you, Father."

"Disturb me? You are why I am here, and by the way, I am not a Priest so you don't have to call me Father unless you want to."

The Chaplain moved to the pew in front of Sam and turned his body to the rear so he and Sam were face to face. He had such a naturally inviting and calming demeanor that Sam began to tell him the full story of his family's struggles. He told the story, in all of its detail, including the accident, the loss of his boys, his amnesia, Sammy's suicide attempt and Laura's request for personal space.

As Sam relayed the story the elderly man looked on attentively. Sam's version of the story was filled with detail, but not judgment or blame. It was also without an onset of emotion. Sam's storytelling felt so cathartic that he didn't have the urge to break down like he did when he was talking to Laura about their painful separation.

"So that is how I ended up here, with you, Father."

"Sam, may I call you Sam?"

"Yes, of course."

Sam realized that he had not told this man his name, yet he knew it. He presumed, like the guard, that he had seen the story on the news.

"Sam, I am so sorry for the pain you and your family are in and I am sorry for the loss of Noah and Jonah."

Again, he knew the names of the boys. How? Had to be the papers or television.

"Sam, the question of why innocent men, women, and children suffer is not a new one. It has been asked by people as long as they have roamed the Earth."

"The Old Testament is filled with stories of the suffering of innocents. The Bible book of your own namesake, Job, is all about suffering. Why did the Israelites suffer at the hands of Pharoah? Why did six million Jews suffer at the hands of the Hitler in the Holocaust? Why did the people of Kalavryta suffer at the hands of the Nazis? What was the justification for three thousand people dying on 9/11? What did Etan Patz, a child, do to deserve to die? Jonah? Noah? What crime could they have committed to warrant their death?"

"Tell me Father. Help me understand."

"Sam the simple and honest answer is 'I don't know'. Anyone who purports to know is either lying, misguided, or privy to more information than me on the subject."

"I'll tell you what I don't believe. I don't believe these are the acts of a willful, spiteful, and vengeful God. I don't believe these are acts of punishment from an angry, Judgment administering God. I also don't believe they are the acts of an uncaring God or a powerless God. I don't believe that God doesn't feel the pain of the world when these tragedies occur."

"So what then?" Sam asked begging for an answer to his questions about the loss of his innocent boys.

"Some say suffering is just part of the natural order of things, Sam. Suffering, pain, sickness. It all helps us to appreciate joy, happiness, and health. Without one we can never truly understand, or appreciate, the other."

"Is that what you believe?"

"Well. While I think it is true, I don't necessarily see it as causal. We do understand joy because it is the absence of sadness, but I am not sure the suffering of an innocent child is required to understand the difference."

"So, what then."

"Sam. I don't honestly know all the answers. I just know this. Suffering is a very real part of the human existence. It always has been. It always will be. It comes in so many forms there is no panacea that can cure it all. We have to accept that it exists. We have to try to minimize it in our lives and do what we can to minimize it in the lives of others, whether they are strangers or loved ones."

"Do you love God, Sam?"

"Yes, I do."

He said without hesitation. Through all of this, while he was confused by God, while he was angry with God, questioned the love God had for him and his family, he never considered that he didn't love God.

"*Sometimes, Sam,* **love isn't always about understanding it is about trusting**."

Sam was shocked a little that the Chaplain used that expression. This was exactly what he was thinking when he decided to consent to Laura's request for a separation and to let go and trust in Laura's love for him in this choice she was making.

"*Faith is hard sometimes, but it is making the choice to trust in God. It is the conscious understanding that God gave us the ability to question everything in our existence, yet did not provide an accompanying book of answers, per se. That is not easy. That* creates anger and abandonment of God and I understand that, completely."

"Listen Sam. Some say it's easy to love God when your life is good, but not so easy when we suffer. I disagree."

"How so?"

"When all of this suffering occurs Sam we can choose to turn our backs on God. I get that. For me I can not."

"Why?"

"Not because it isn't hard to love God when we face suffering, but because in suffering I see no other choice. When I look at all of those innocent lives lost and in pain I refuse to believe they died in vain. When I look at the lives of Jonah and Noah I refuse to believe they are not in a better place, with God, in no pain. I refuse to believe they are not in a place with no discomfort. I refuse to believe they are not in a place with no sickness. I refuse to believe they are not in a place with no inhumanity."

"Sam, when I look at the lives of your four year old angels I refuse to believe, if I am you, that I will not be joined with them in the afterlife in the joy and in the comfort of the loving God that I believe in. If not for believing that Sam I could not face the alternatives. That your boys died in vain? That your boys are not in a better place? That you will never see them again? I refuse to accept it Sam."

"I have no choice but to trust in God's plan and God's love."

"So what does all this mean for you Sam. It doesn't mean you don't question. It doesn't mean you don't wave your fist in anger at the Lord and rebel sometimes. It means that you go on with your life in the loving memory or your boys. It means that you do everything you can to live your life to the fullest and to honor their memory. It means, Sam, that you do everything you can for every day of your life to alleviate the suffering of those that you care about."

Sam was overwhelmed by the deeply impassioned words coming out of the mouth of this seemingly quiet, old preacher. The message resonated soundly with Sam. For the first time since he awoke, he didn't feel so alone. He didn't feel so without direction and purpose. For the first time since he awoke, he felt a measure of hope.

"You are a good man, Sam Job. You have a good wife and family. Despite it all you are going to be okay. Keep living your life as fully and completely as you are able. Never forget the healing power of God's unconditional love, Sam Job. Even in your darkest hours always know God is with you and loves you. That will honor your boys."

Just then Laura peered her head through the open door of the Chapel.

"Sorry to disturb you Sam, but the doctor said we can see Sammy in a few minutes. I figured you wanted to join me."

"Thanks Laura."

He turned to thank the Chaplain and introduce Laura when he realized he was alone in the Chapel. He surveyed the room and there was no one there but him, aside from Laura. He scanned for an exit door and realized there was none. There was only the door that Laura had entered the Chapel through. Sam froze for a moment, but, oddly, didn't feel any sense of panic. He knew he didn't imagine the whole thing. He also knew that he couldn't explain it. He didn't need to. He got the message. He understood.

"Everything alright, Sam?"

"Yes, let's go see Sammy."

He moved towards Laura and went to take her hand.

"Is that okay?" he asked.

"Yes, Sam, of course."

They walked hand in hand towards the door of the Chapel. As they did Sam looked back over the room a final time to make sure he wasn't mistaken about the Exit. He was not. The Chapel was empty and they were leaving through the only door. They crossed the threshold towards Sammy's room. As they did the Chapel door closed behind them. On the backside of the Chapel door was a small faded plaque. The plaque reads:

"This Chapel is dedicated to the loving memory of Chaplain Robert Strong (1905-1986) killed in a pedestrian auto accident in front of this hospital."

Etched in the plaque was a photo of the deceased Chaplain with his balding head, thick glasses, kindly smile, and neatly trimmed goatee.

THE END